This book belongs to:

The Princess
of Pink
Treasury

Pinkalicious™

The Princess of Pink Treasury

by Victoria Kann

HARPER

An Imprint of HarperCollinsPublishers

The author gratefully acknowledges
the artistic and editorial contributions
of Natalie Engel, Justine Fontes,
Barry Gott, Daniel Griffo, Susan Hill,
Robert Masheris, and Michael Teitelbaum.

Pinkalicious: The Princess of Pink Treasury

Copyright © 2006, 2007, 2009, 2010, 2011 by Victoria Kann, Inc.

PINKALICIOUS and all related logos and characters
are trademarks of Victoria Kann, Inc. Used with permission.

Based on the HarperCollins book *Pinkalicious* written by
Victoria Kann and Elizabeth Kann, illustrated by Victoria Kann

For information address HarperCollins Children's Books,
a division of HarperCollins Publishers, 10 East 53rd Street, New York, NY 10022.
www.harpercollinschildrens.com

Library of Congress catalog card number: 2011929313
ISBN 978-0-06-210236-2

Book design by John Sazaklis and Theresa Venezia

12   13   14   15   CG/RRDC   10   9   8   7   6   5   4   3
❖
Previously published separately as *School Rules!*, *Pinkalicious and the Pink Drink*,
Pink around the Rink, *Tickled Pink*, and *Pinkie Promise*.

For my treasured team,
Tamar, John, and Kirsten,
who help make it all happen!
—V.K.

Table of Contents

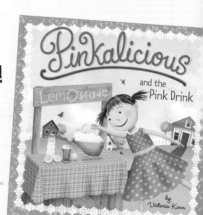

Pinkalicious

School Rules!

by Victoria Kann

To Zelda, Grace, and David
—V.K.

The author gratefully acknowledges
the artistic and editorial contributions
of Daniel Griffo and Susan Hill.

Pinkalicious: School Rules!
Copyright © 2010 by Victoria Kann, Inc.

PINKALICIOUS and all related logos and characters are trademarks of Victoria Kann, Inc. Used with permission.

Based on the HarperCollins book *Pinkalicious* written by
Victoria Kann and Elizabeth Kann, illustrated by Victoria Kann

For information address HarperCollins Children's Books, a division of HarperCollins Publishers,
10 East 53rd Street, New York, NY 10022.
www.icanread.com

Library of Congress catalog card number: 2009053452
❖

Pinkalicious™

School Rules!

by Victoria Kann

School is okay.

Except for one thing.

When I am at school,

I miss Goldilicious.

Goldie, for short.

Goldie is my unicorn.

I really like my teacher.

His name is Mr. Pushkin.

I have some friends in my class
and I made a new friend yesterday.
But I miss Goldie anyway.

This morning when I woke up

I had a very good idea.

I could bring Goldie to school with me!

School would be
perfectly pinkatastic
with Goldilicious
there, too.

There was a shiny red apple
on Mr. Pushkin's desk.

Goldie took the apple
and nibbled it gently.

Mr. Pushkin heard Goldie munching
and he thought it was me.
"Pinkalicious, there is no eating
until snack time," he said.
"It's the rule."

"It's not me," I said.

"It's Goldilicious, my unicorn!

She didn't eat much for breakfast,"
I added.

Mr. Pushkin smiled.

He took me aside

and he told me that unicorns

are not allowed in school.

"It's the rule," he said.

Rules are something

I do not love about school.

And I really do not love

the rule about no unicorns.

I began to cry a little.

I cried a little harder.

"Okay, Pinkalicious,"

said Mr. Pushkin.

"Your unicorn may stay,

just this once."

I stopped crying.

In fact, I clapped and twirled.

"But if your unicorn stays, you must teach her the rules," Mr. Pushkin said. "Do you think you can do that?"

"Yes!" I said.

"I know I can!"

At reading time,

Goldilicious was very quiet.

Goldilicious helped me with my math.

Unicorns are very good at counting.

When it was time for recess,

I showed Goldilicious

how to line up by the door.

Goldilicious did not push

or wiggle or cut the line at all.

Goldilicious played nicely

with the other kids.

Everyone had so much fun
with Goldie and me.

I didn't know I had

so many friends at school!

Soon it was time to go home.

Goldie got my backpack

off its hook.

"Tell me, Pinkalicious,"

said Mr. Pushkin.

"Did you and your unicorn

have a good day?"

"We sure did!" I said.

"School rules!"

This way to find some things that really rule!

Pinkalicious Jump Rope Rhymes

Pinkalicious likes to jump rope. Here are some of her favorite jump rope rhymes for you to try!

Chant this to the same rhythm as "Teddy Bear." If the jumper manages to mime each action and jump out of the rope at the end without missing, she gets another turn!

Pinkalicious, Pinkalicious,
do a twirl
Pinkalicious, Pinkalicious,
string a pearl
Pinkalicious, Pinkalicious,
give a clap
Pinkalicious, Pinkalicious,
take a nap
Pinkalicious, Pinkalicious,
tie your shoes
Pinkalicious, Pinkalicious,
read the news
Pinkalicious, Pinkalicious,
don't ask why
Pinkalicious, Pinkalicious,
wave good-bye!

Goldilicious, Goldilicious, gallop around
Goldilicious, Goldilicious, stomp the ground
Goldilicious, Goldilicious, shake your horn
Goldilicious, Goldilicious, eat some corn

Goldilicious, Goldilicious, do a dance
Goldilicious, Goldilicious, skip and prance
Goldilicious, Goldilicious, give a cheer
Goldilicious, Goldilicious, disappear!

Bubblegum, bubblegum, pink and sweet
Bubblegum's my favorite treat
Blow a bubble to the sky,
Blow it bigger than a pie!
Bubblegum, bubblegum, sweet and pink
Jump until you just can't think.
Chew until your chewers ache
And you have to take a break!

Pinkalicious walks like this
Pinkalicious talks like this
Pinkalicious twirls like this
Pinkalicious throws a kiss!

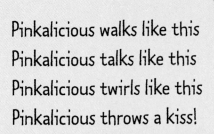

Here are some counting rhymes!

Pinkalicious lost a tooth,
Then she acted like a goof!
How many fairies did she offend?
Keep on jumping till the end!
One, two, three ...

Pinkalicious dressed in pink
Made some lemonade to drink.
How many lemons did she use?
One, two, three ...

Pinkalicious in the rink,
Skated till the ice turned pink.
How many times did she fall down?
One, two, three ...

Pinkalicious, Pinkalicious, bubblegum—POP!
How many bubbles before I stop?
One, two, three ...

Follow the actions described when you jump to these rhymes:

Pinkalicious went to town
to buy pink shoes and a pink gown
Her brother Peter stayed home in bed
To read a book; here's what it said:
"Close your eyes and count to ten.
If you miss, you take a jump rope end."

Pinkalicious went to France
To teach the ladies how to dance.
First the heel, then the toe,
Twirl around, and out you go!

This rhyme gives you an answer,
depending on when you miss.

Bake pink cupcakes, mix and blend.
Tell me the name of my best friend:
A, B, C, D . . .

Make a New Friend!

**Pinkalicious makes lots of friends at school.
Here are some good tips for making a new friend!**

💗 **Say hello!** The first step is always to greet your new friend! Find out your new friend's name and make sure to introduce yourself.

💗 **Ask questions!** Ask your friend about something that they like or ask them if they are interested in one of your own favorite things! Any question will get your new friend talking in no time.

💗 **Show your new friend something pinkerrific!** Show your new friend something special to you—your favorite food, favorite toy, even a picture of a pet or family member. Sharing is always a good way to make new friends.

💗 **Invite your friend to do something with you!** Ask your new friend to come to your house after school. You can also ask your friend to join in on an activity at school or a game you always play at recess. Get creative!

Be Imaginative!

Pinkalicious has an imaginary friend, Goldilicious.
Do you have an imaginary friend?
If not, you can make one up!
Look inside the frame below and imagine what your friend looks like.
Now, on a separate piece of paper, draw or collage a picture of your friend.

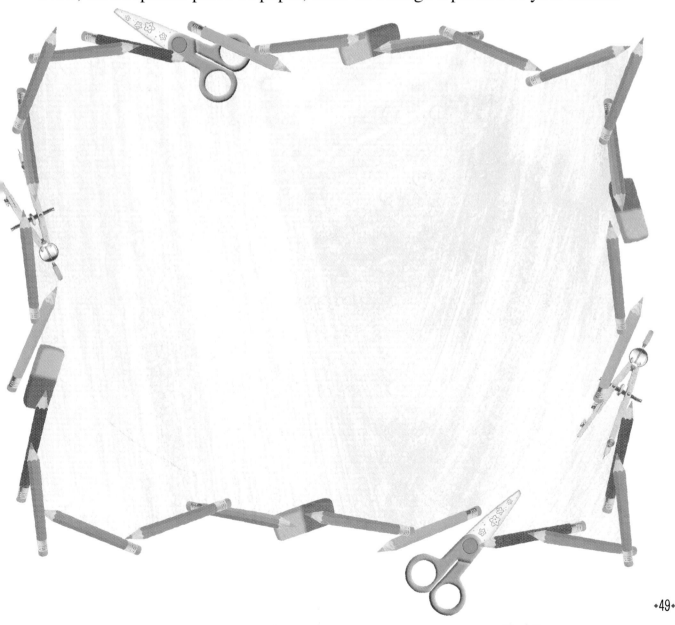

Spot the Differences:
Cubby Commotion

Can you find 5 differences between the 2 pictures?

Answers: 1. Color of the far left bag 2. Color of cubbies 3. Pink bag is missing from Goldilicious's horn 4. Flower in Pinkalicious's hair 5. Classmate's mouth

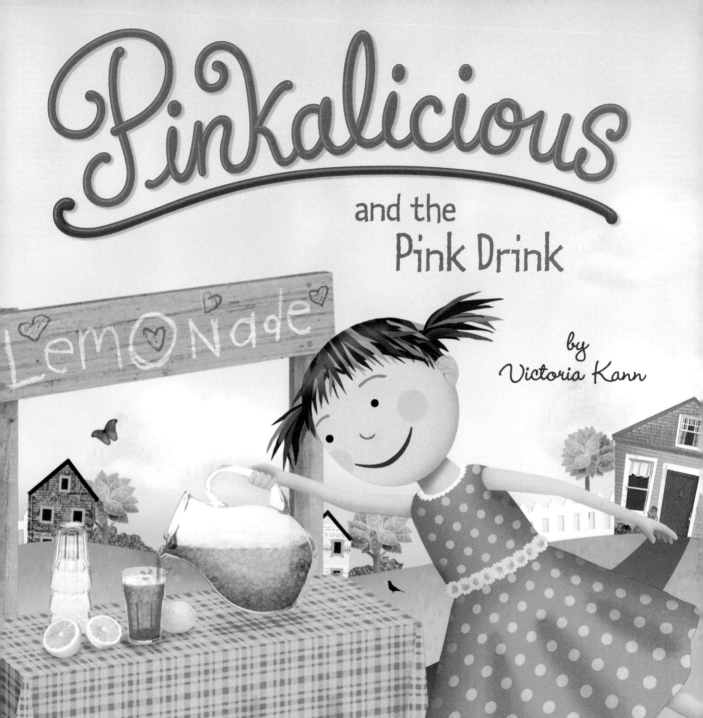

Pinkalicious

and the
Pink Drink

by
Victoria Kann

To Sallie
—V.K.

The author gratefully acknowledges
the artistic and editorial contributions
of Barry Gott and Susan Hill.

Pinkalicious: Pinkalicious and the Pink Drink
Copyright © 2010 by Victoria Kann, Inc.

PINKALICIOUS and all related logos and characters
are trademarks of Victoria Kann, Inc. Used with permission.

Based on the HarperCollins book *Pinkalicious* written by
Victoria Kann and Elizabeth Kann, illustrated by Victoria Kann

For information address HarperCollins Children's Books,
a division of HarperCollins Publishers, 10 East 53rd Street, New York, NY 10022.
www.harpercollinschildrens.com

Library of Congress catalog card number: 2009941833
❖

It was a sunny day, too hot to play.
I was blowing bubbles in the shade.

That made me think of the giant bubblegum machine at the toy store. I ran inside to check my piggy bank.

It was empty!

I wanted a gumball. I wanted twenty gumballs. I wanted thirty-five gumballs, pink ones!

But how could I get the money to buy them?

Mommy said, "Let's have a lemonade stand!"
"Pink lemonade!" I said. "Pink, pink, pink!"
Mommy got out the pitcher and the sugar and the lemons.
"I know how!" I said. "I'll do it myself!"

I put the sugar and the water into the pitcher.
I squeezed the lemons. I stirred it all together.
It was yummy. But it wasn't pink.

I opened the fridge. I didn't find any pink lemons, but I found some other pinkish things: pink grapefruit, pink watermelon, pink frosting, and a bowlful of purplicious beets.

I put all of them in the pitcher and I stirred it all up.

My little brother, Peter, helped me put up my pink lemonade stand. I let him try the lemonade for free.

"Weird," said Peter. "Kind of chewy. I like it."

Mr. Peabody came by and gave me a quarter.

My first real customer!

Mr. Peabody made a face. "It's definitely missing something," he said. "Either that, or it has too much of something else."

I had an idea. "The sweeter, the better," I said.
I ran and got the honey bear and squeezed the honey in.
Peter stirred and—oh no! He knocked over the pitcher!
"I'm sorry, Pinkalicious!" he said. "Don't get mad!"

I got mad.

"That's easy to fix, Pinkalicious. We'll make some more," said Mommy.

I started to get out the pink grapefruit, pink watermelon, pink frosting, and purplicious beets.

"What's all that?" Mommy asked.

"All that's how to make it pink," I told her.

Mommy said, "How about we just use one thing to make it pink this time." And she pulled out some strawberries.

It wasn't as exciting or as lumpy as the first batch, but it was still beautiful pink lemonade. I sold the whole pitcher in no time flat.

I went to the toy store with my lemonade stand money. Six quarters, four dimes, five nickels, and ten pennies.

Nine gumballs, pink ones! Eight for me and one for Peter.

Peter looked sad. I gave him three and kept six. Peter still looked sad. I stuffed one gumball in my mouth, kept four, and gave four to Peter. "Even-Steven!" Peter said. He was very happy.

Gumballs don't last forever, and my piggy bank is empty again.

Maybe tomorrow I'll have a bake sale. I can make pink cupcakes.

Something's bubbling
in the kitchen!
This way to find out
what's cooking....

Pink Lemonade for All!

Make Your Own Lemonade Stand

It takes more than lemonade to make a lemonade stand—especially a perfectly Pinkalicious one! Here are some suggestions for making an outstanding stand.

💜 You can turn any sturdy cardboard box or wooden crate into a lemonade stand. If possible, paint your stand pink!

💜 Use pink markers, glitter, ribbons, and glue to create a big sign for the front of your stand. You might also want to make some pink flyers to put up around your neighborhood and school to let people know where they can get the best pink lemonade around.

A Pinkatastic Place for Your Silver and Green

You'll need change for your customers and a place to stow your profits. Why settle for an ordinary cash box when you can have a Pinkalicious one?

💜 Decorate an old lunch box with pink ribbons. Use pink muffin papers to create separate compartments for quarters, dimes, nickels, and pennies. Put paper money in an envelope, but don't forget to mark the front!

💜 Make sure you have some change before your stand opens—in case someone wants to buy lemonade but only has a ten-dollar bill.

Pinkalicious Lemonade

Start with frozen lemonade or follow these directions to make about 2 1/2 quarts of pinkalicious lemonade!

You will need:

- **8** cups of water
- **2** cups sugar
- **2 1/4** cups lemon juice
- **2** cups ice
- **3/4** cup crushed frozen strawberries

Directions:

Be sure and have a grown-up help you with anything involving the stove, the oven, or the blender!

- Put one cup of water into a pot and bring it to a boil.
- Add sugar to boiling water, and stir until all the sugar is dissolved.
- Take the sugar water off the stove, and add all of the lemon juice.
- Put 7 cups of cold water and 2 cups of ice into a pitcher. When sugar water has cooled, add to the pitcher.
- Crushed frozen strawberries can be added to the pitcher until you reach your desired pinkness!

To make your Pinkalicious lemonade pinkerrific, serve it in pink cups with pink straws! And for that perfectly pink drink, freeze maraschino cherries or fresh raspberries in ice-cube trays so even your ice cubes are pretty!

Pink-a-Yummy Cookies

If you're looking to add something extra to your lemonade stand, try for some pinkatastic cookies! It's easy to turn any batch of sugar cookies pink by boiling beets, then adding the pink water to the dough. Or you can use strawberry cake mix to create these quick cookies. Ask a grown-up to work the oven and electric mixer.

You will need:

- 2 eggs
- 2/3 cup shortening
- 1 box of strawberry cake mix

Optional: strawberry frosting with any of the
following mixed in: sprinkles or
sugar crystals, either pink or red

Directions:
Be sure to have a grown-up help you with anything
involving the stove, the oven, or the blender!

- Preheat oven to 375 degrees.
- In a medium-sized mixing bowl, beat eggs and shortening.
- Gradually beat in cake mix until completely blended.
- Use your hands to form one-inch balls.
- Place on ungreased baking sheet.
- Bake 10 to 12 minutes.
- Let cool on sheet for 2 minutes before moving
  to a cooling rack.
- If wanted, when completely cool, frost with pink frosting
  and dust with pink sprinkles or colored sugar, or top
  with another cookie to make sandwiches!

Fairy Catcher Fun!

Take a close look at how Pinkalicious appears on this page.
What is she holding? What is she wearing? Now look at the picture on the next page.
Which one matches Pinkalicious?

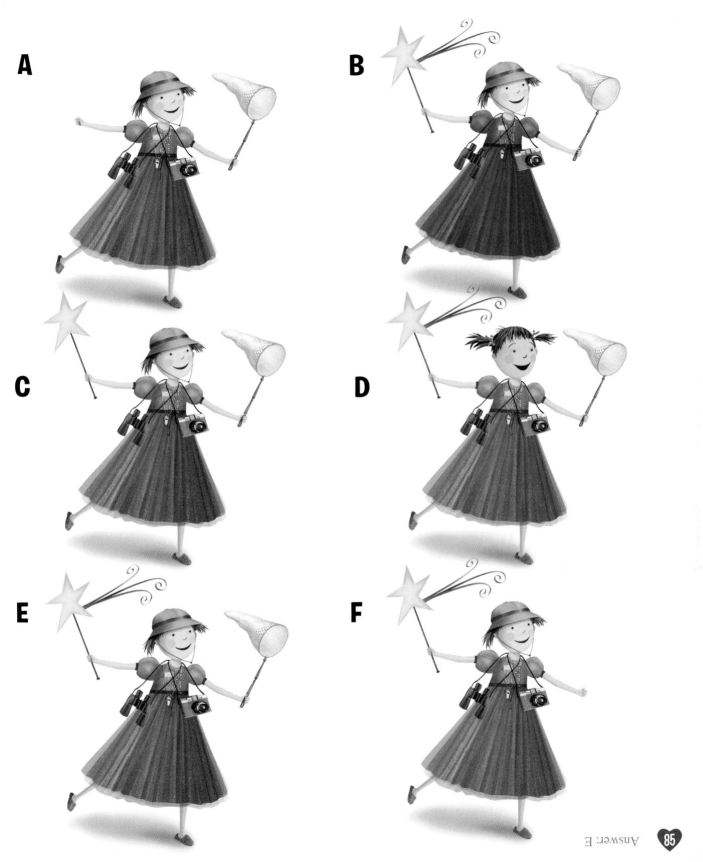

A

B

C

D

E

F

Answer: E

Spot the Differences:
Stand Switcheroo

Can you find 7 differences between the 2 pictures?

Pinkalicious

Pink around the Rink

by
Victoria Kann

To Maeve, Gareth, Nancy, and Kevin
—V.K.

The author gratefully acknowledges
the artistic and editorial contributions
of Daniel Griffo and Susan Hill.

Pinkalicious: Pink around the Rink
Copyright © 2010 by Victoria Kann, Inc.

PINKALICIOUS and all related logos and characters
are trademarks of Victoria Kann, Inc. Used with permission.

Based on the HarperCollins book *Pinkalicious* written by
Victoria Kann and Elizabeth Kann, illustrated by Victoria Kann

For information address HarperCollins Children's Books, a division of HarperCollins Publishers,
10 East 53rd Street, New York, NY 10022.
www.icanread.com

Library of Congress catalog card number: 2010012633
❖

Pink around the Rink

by Victoria Kann

Yesterday,

Mommy gave me a big surprise.

It was a pair of brand-new

ice skates!

"Do you like them?" Mommy asked.

"I like them," I told her.

But there was one thing I did not like.

My new skates were not pink.

They were not purple,

or blue, or even green.

My new skates were boring old white.

"I can fix that," I said to myself.

I got my markers.

I picked out the color called

cotton candy pink,

and I colored my skates all over.

I was very careful.

Ta-da!

They looked pinkatastic.

Now I loved my new skates.
And I loved how I looked
in my new skates.

I couldn't wait

to go to the rink.

I would glide and spin.

I would be so graceful

in my cotton candy skates.

We went to the rink
the very next day.

"Your skates!" said Mommy.

"They're pink!" said Daddy.

"Cotton candy pink," I said.

I smiled.

Mommy did not
exactly smile.
Daddy smiled a little,
I think.

"Ready?" asked Daddy.

"Ready!" I said.

I was ready

to glide and spin!

I was not ready to wobble and fall.

But that is what I did.

I wobbled and fell again and again
and again.

Ouch!

But my sore bottom

wasn't the worst part.

The worst part was that

every time I fell,

my cotton candy skates

left cotton candy spots

and streaks all over the ice.

Everyone saw.

I started to cry a little.

Okay, a lot.

"Are you all right?" Mommy asked.

"I cry when something hurts, too,"

Daddy said.

"It's not that," I wailed.

"Look!" I pointed at my trail

of cotton candy pink

and my wet, messy skates.

Mommy smiled at me.

"The ice is pretty.

And your skates are one of a kind,

Pinkalicious," she said.

"Just like you."

I looked at my skates again.
Shades of pink dripped
and swirled and swooped
all over them.

Mommy was right.

My skates looked fantastic.

I was ready to try again.

Daddy skated with me
and held on to my hand.
This time I didn't
wobble and fall.
I was very graceful!

"That was fun!"

I said when

we got home.

"I'm glad," said Mommy,
"because I signed you up
for skating lessons!"

My new skates and I can hardly wait
to go skating again!

Slide and glide
to the next page
to spin
into some
spectacular
activities!

Entertaining Outdoor Winter Activities!

Pinkalicious Snow Parade

Fashion a flag to carry by tying a pink scarf or banner to an umbrella (feel free to add ribbons). Gather a few friends and put on your warmest, pinkest clothes. Step outside and form a line. Take turns being the leader and holding up your flag to wave in the wind.

Pretend you are unicorns, fairies, or prancing princesses. Do your best to leave magical footprints in the snow.

When your cheeks get too pink, go inside for hot chocolate. Or if you prefer—warm pink milk (just use strawberry syrup instead of chocolate).

Pink Snow Fairies

It's fun to make snow fairies—and even more fun to turn them pink! Fill a squeeze bottle (like an empty plastic ketchup or mustard bottle) with water dyed using drops of red food coloring.

Then go outside in the snow. Lie on your back and move your arms and legs up and down to form a snow fairy.

Stand up and squirt red liquid on your fairy to outline her wings, or draw pretty designs on her skirt.

You can also make snow angels and snow butterflies. Or just use your squeeze bottle to draw anything in the snow—like pink unicorns, pink poodles, giant pink cupcakes, or... Pinkalicious!

Amusing Indoor Winter Activities!

A Sweet Treat for Your Tweets!

Everyone loves a snack—including our feathered friends! During the winter, it's harder for birds to find seeds to snack on, so help them out with this fun activity.

What you'll need:

- A pinecone
- String
- Peanut butter
- Bird seed
- A paper plate

Directions:

- Take the pinecone and brush off any dirt or snow that may have gotten stuck. Peanut butter will stick better on a clean pinecone.

- Tie a string to the top part of your pinecone. Make sure it's on securely—this will hold the pinecone treat upright while the birds are snacking!

- Spread peanut butter all over the pinecone. Make sure to cover the whole cone, from top to bottom!

- Spread a layer of seeds onto your paper plate.

- Roll the peanut butter–covered pinecone in the seed dish, making sure that the seeds stick to the peanut butter.

- Hang your seeded treat in a tree to share the snack!

Indoor Skating Rink

Some days you can't get out to the skating rink. But you can still have plenty of fun twirling around!

Find or clear a space free of furniture in your house. Arrange a big loop of pink yarn on the floor to create your indoor skating rink. Play skating music, like waltzes or ballets.

Put on a tutu or skating skirt. (If you don't have one, just tie a pretty pink scarf around your waist.)

Now twirl around your rink. See how graceful you can be. Find a short piece of music you like and choreograph an ice dance to it.

Ask your friends to come over for the Pinkalympics! Every friend can have cards with the numbers 1 through 10 on them, so that they can vote on the best performances. It's a perfect score!

Find the Hidden Hearts

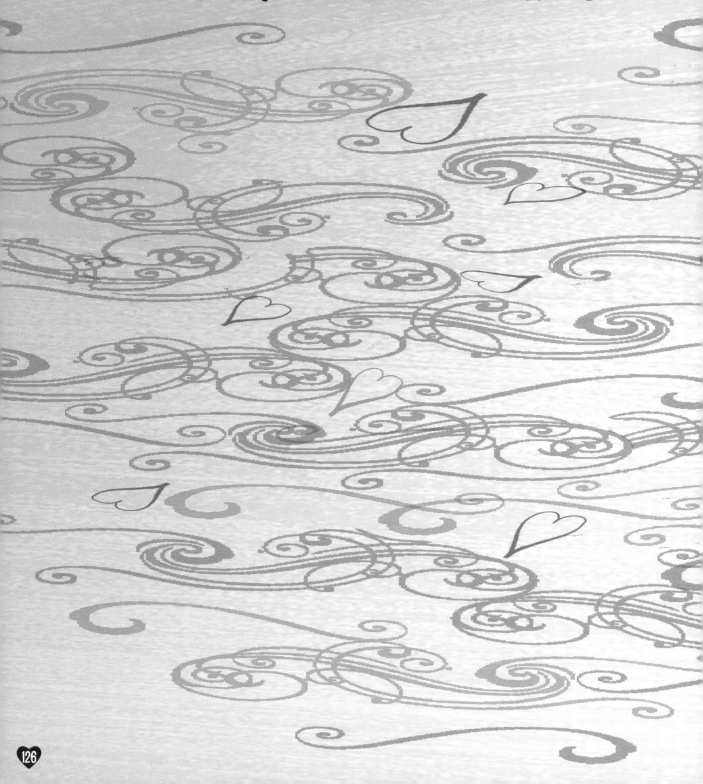

**Pinkalicious's pink skates have left hearts hidden in the swirls!
How many can you find?**

Answer: There are 15 hearts!

Spot the Differences:
Ice Princess Puzzler

Can you find 6 differences between the 2 pictures?

Pinkalicious

Tickled Pink

by Victoria Kann

For Margaret, Michael, Wes, and Carly,
you tickle me pink!
—V.K.

The author gratefully acknowledges
the artistic and editorial contributions
of Bob Masheris and Natalie Engel.

I was in the library, looking for a good book.

giggle giggle

ha ha ha ha

I poked around the shelves until I found something with a bright pink cover and shiny gold letters.
The Goofy Book of Gags and Giggles, I read.
I opened it up.

It was full of hilarious jokes! I started reading and giggling. I bit my lip to try to keep from laughing out loud, but the jokes were too funny.

I checked the book out and put it in my backpack until recess.

giggle ha ha

ha ha

The Goofy Book of Gags and Giggles

giggle giggle

When it was finally time to go outside, I took the book with me.

"What are you reading, Pinkalicious?" Molly asked.

"A joke book I found," I said. "Listen to this:
Where do cows go on a first date?
To the MOOvies!"

The Goofy Book of Gags and Giggles

Molly couldn't stop laughing. We laughed so hard that Alex and Alison came over to see what was going on.

"Pinkalicious has a joke book," said Molly. "Go ahead, Pinkalicious, read them another one."

"Okay," I said. "Why do birds fly south in the winter?"

"Why?" said Alex, Molly, and Alison.

"Because it's too far to walk!" I said.

We giggled until our tummies hurt. I told them another joke and another. Soon everyone was listening to us.

"Pinkalicious, you're hilarious!" one kid said, laughing.

"No she's not," said Tiffany, who was listening the whole time. "Anyone can be funny if they're reading from a book. I bet Pinkalicious doesn't have a real funny bone in her body."

"I do, too!" I shouted, my cheeks turning pink with anger.

"Prove it," said Tiffany. She challenged me to a laugh-off for the next day.

"You can tell any joke you want, but you have to make it up yourself," she said.

I wasn't sure I could think of a joke as good as the ones in my book, but I agreed. Everyone was watching. What else could I do?

That night, I told my family about my dilemma.

"I need to create a joke that's fizzier than pink lemonade, more fun than pink cupcakes, more pinkatastic than pink!" I said. "It has to be the most pinkerrifically funny joke of all time."

"Hey, Pinkalicious. I have a joke," said Peter. "Knock, knock."

"Who's there?"

"Pinky, stinky underwear!" Peter practically laughed himself right off his chair.

"Yuck, Peter," I said. "NOT funny. Not funny at all."

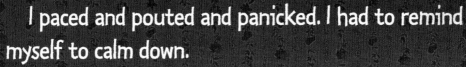

I paced and pouted and panicked. I had to remind myself to calm down.

"Think pink," I said, "and the answer will follow."

In the middle of the night, I had an idea. Maybe, just maybe, it would be good enough to win.

The next morning, I had trouble swallowing my cereal. My stomach felt funny all during school. Then, at last, the big moment came.

"It's time for the laugh-off," yelled Alex. "First up is Tiffany."

Tiffany strutted up to the jungle gym.

"What's black and white and red all over?" she said.

"An embarrassed zebra?" someone said.

"No," Tiffany said.

"A sunburned skunk?"

"No."

"What?"

"A PENGUIN WHO ATE ALL THE PINK CUPCAKES!"

Everybody laughed. I was going to lose, big time.

I was next, and I was worried. My joke had seemed funny in the middle of the night, but it didn't seem all that funny now. *What if nobody gets it? What if nobody laughs?* I thought.

"What's the matter, Pinkalicious?" yelled Tiffany. "Can't you be funny without your book?"

I walked over to the jungle gym. I looked at all the kids looking at me. My mouth felt dry. I swallowed. *Oh well*, I thought, *even if my joke isn't the best, at least everyone will know it's my own.*

"What's even funnier than being tickled?" I said.

"BEING TICKLED PINK!" I cried. I tickled people until they laughed so hard their faces turned bright pink. Everyone was laughing—even Tiffany.

"Okay, Pinkalicious," she said. "I guess you do have a funny bone after all."

"Thanks." I smiled with relief. "I liked your joke, too."

After the laugh-off, I returned the joke book to the library. Now that it was over, nothing seemed quite as funny as being tickled pink!

Giggles galore—right ahead!

Jokes to Tickle You Pink!

Here are some hilarious jokes to share with a friend—or to laugh on your own!

Which fingers would Pinkalicious use to finger paint?

Her pinkies!

ha ha   ha ha

If you had one pink cupcake and your friend had two pink cupcakes, how many pink cupcakes would you both have?

None! Because they're so sweetalicious, you'd eat them all up!

Knock, knock
Who's there?
Pink-a.
Pink-a who?
Pink-a-boo, I see you!

What did the pink ice-cream cone say to the purple ice-cream cone?

Nothing. Ice-cream cones can't talk, silly!

Of all the days—Monday, Tuesday, Wednesday, Thursday, Friday, Saturday, or Sunday—which is best?

A Pinkalicious Day, of course!

Knock, knock
Who's there?
Pink.
Pink who?
I pink I really like purple.

giggle

giggle giggle

The Goofy Book of Gags and Giggles

Did you hear about the pink cow?

She gave strawberry-flavored milk!

Be a Pinkerrific Joke Teller!

So you love jokes. But maybe you're a little nervous about telling jokes. Will they be funny? Will you tell them right?

No worries. Here are some tips on how to be a pinkerrific joke teller!

- **Practice! Practice! Practice!** Practicing makes the difference.

- **Rehearse your jokes in front of a mirror.** Stand in front of a full-length mirror so you can see what you look like when you're telling your joke. What expression do you have on your face? What are you doing with your hands? When you tell your friends a joke they are not only listening to you— they are looking at you as well.

- **Write the jokes down.** There is no rule that says you have to memorize your jokes! Jokes can be just as funny if you read them.

- **Decide what you think is funny.** If you don't think a joke is funny, you probably shouldn't tell that joke. If you do think it's a funny joke, go ahead and practice telling it, then make your friends and family giggle!

Have Your Own Laugh-off

You and your friends can have a laugh-off just like Pinkalicious and her friends. How? It's easy!

- **Invite your friends over.** Ask each friend to write his or her favorite joke on a piece of paper and bring it along. Write your own favorite joke down on a piece of paper, too.

- **Don't read any of the jokes!** Not yet, anyway. Fold up the papers with the jokes and toss them into a hat or a bowl or a bag. Shake the hat, bowl, or bag, so that the papers get all scrambled up.

- **One by one, have each of your friends pull out a piece of paper and read the joke on that paper.** It may be the joke that they brought, or it may be a joke that someone else brought. Go around until all of the jokes have been read.

You can turn your laugh-off into a game! After each joke is read, have everyone guess who brought it. For each right guess, you get a point. When all the jokes have been read, add up the points to see who wins the game. Happy laughing!

Write Your Own Pinkatastic Story!

Anyone can make a book. You just need the right ingredients: Characters, settings, story, words, and (sometimes) pictures.

First decide how long you want your book to be: 8, 16, 24, or 32 pages? (You might want to start small and work your way up to longer books.)

Staple or stitch some blank pieces of paper together. Soon you will be ready to draw the cover, write the title, and then fill those pages with your very own story. But first you need to make some choices. These lists will help you decide.

Pink is still perfect.

Who's who?
Who is your hero or heroine?
- ☐ Pinkalicious?
- ☐ Peter?
- ☐ You?
- ☐ Someone you know?
- ☐ A character whose name and qualities you make up?

Who else is in the story?
- ☐ Friends?
- ☐ Family?
- ☐ Teachers?
- ☐ Butterflies?
- ☐ Ballerinas?

Where's there? What is the setting for your story?

- ☐ Pinkville?
- ☐ School?
- ☐ Home?
- ☐ A place you've been?
- ☐ Someplace you've only imagined or seen pictures of?

What's happening? What happens to your hero or your heroine?

- ☐ Does the character make a new friend?
- ☐ Does he or she learn something?
- ☐ Does he or she help someone else or get help?

On your mark, get set, start! How will you start your story?

Here are the opening lines from a few Pinkalicious stories to use, or you can make up your own!

- ☐ School is okay. Except for one thing . . .
- ☐ It was a sunny day, too hot to play . . .
- ☐ Yesterday, Mommy gave me a big surprise . . .
- ☐ I was in the library, looking for a good book . . .
- ☐ I was making a picture for my teacher . . .

The finish line

It helps to know how your story will end, even before you start writing. Imagine the whole story in your mind. Then tell the idea to your imaginary friend or someone else you trust. Does it make sense when you say it out loud? Once the story is clear, start writing and drawing pictures.

Fear not!

Don't be afraid to try . . . and try again! If you don't like the way your book turns out at first, just keep writing and drawing until you do. If a picture doesn't come out the way you want, you can always paste another one over it.

Spot the Differences:
Recess Riddle!

Can you find 8 differences between the 2 pictures?

Pinkalicious

Pinkie Promise

by
Victoria
Kann

For Marjorie and Bob,
thank you for your support and guidance.
—V.K.

The author gratefully acknowledges
the artistic and editorial contributions
of Daniel Griffo and Susan Hill.

Pinkie Promise

by Victoria Kann

I was making a picture

for my teacher, Mr. Pushkin.

I ran out of my favorite color.

I asked my friend Alison

if I could borrow her paints.

"Just don't use up all the pink," she said.

"I won't," I said.

"I promise."

I worked very hard on the picture.

It looked good.

I gave the picture to Mr. Pushkin.

"What a terrific painting!" he said.

"It's so pink."

"You mean it's pinkerrific!" I said.

Alison was coming over
to get her paint set.

Some of the colors were empty.

Uh-oh.

What was I going to do?

"Um . . . I'm sorry, Alison," I said.

"By mistake I used up all the pink."

Alison frowned.

"You also used up all the red

and the white," she said.

"Well, red and white make pink,

so really it's all pink," I said.

Alison was angry.

"You said you wouldn't use up
all the pink paint!" said Alison.
"You promised."
"I'm really really sorry, Alison,"
I said again.
Alison took her paint set
and walked away.

Alison did not sit with me at lunch.

I sat alone.

I ate my jelly sandwich.

Jelly does not taste pink-a-yummy

if you are eating all by yourself.

Then I thought of something.

I went back to the classroom.

I made Alison a card to apologize.

"This card is very blue,"

I said to Alison.

"There were no other colors.

Almost everybody is out of pink."

"Thanks for the card," Alison said.

"It's not just beautiful, it's bluetiful."

"Alison," I asked,

"can we still be friends?"

"Of course we're friends,
Pinkalicious," Alison said.
"I'm sorry I got angry
about the paint.
I won't get so mad next time."

I was so happy!

"Let's play this weekend!" I said.

When Alison came over to play,

I had a surprise for her.

I gave Alison a new tube of paint.

"It's not even my birthday!"

said Alison.

"And that's not all," I said.

"Guess what?"

We got ice cream!

We shared a pink peppermint ice cream sundae with raspberry swirl syrup.

The sundae had two cherries on top

so we could each have our own.

Some things are just too hard to share!

PLEASING POMEGRANATE PUNCH

MAGENTA MINT MANGO

PINK PEPPERMINT

PLUM PINK PERFECTION

"Let's always be friends,"
Alison said.
"Yes, that would be funtastic,"
I said.

"Let's make it a pinkie promise!"

we said at the same time.

"Pinkie promises last forever,"

I said happily.

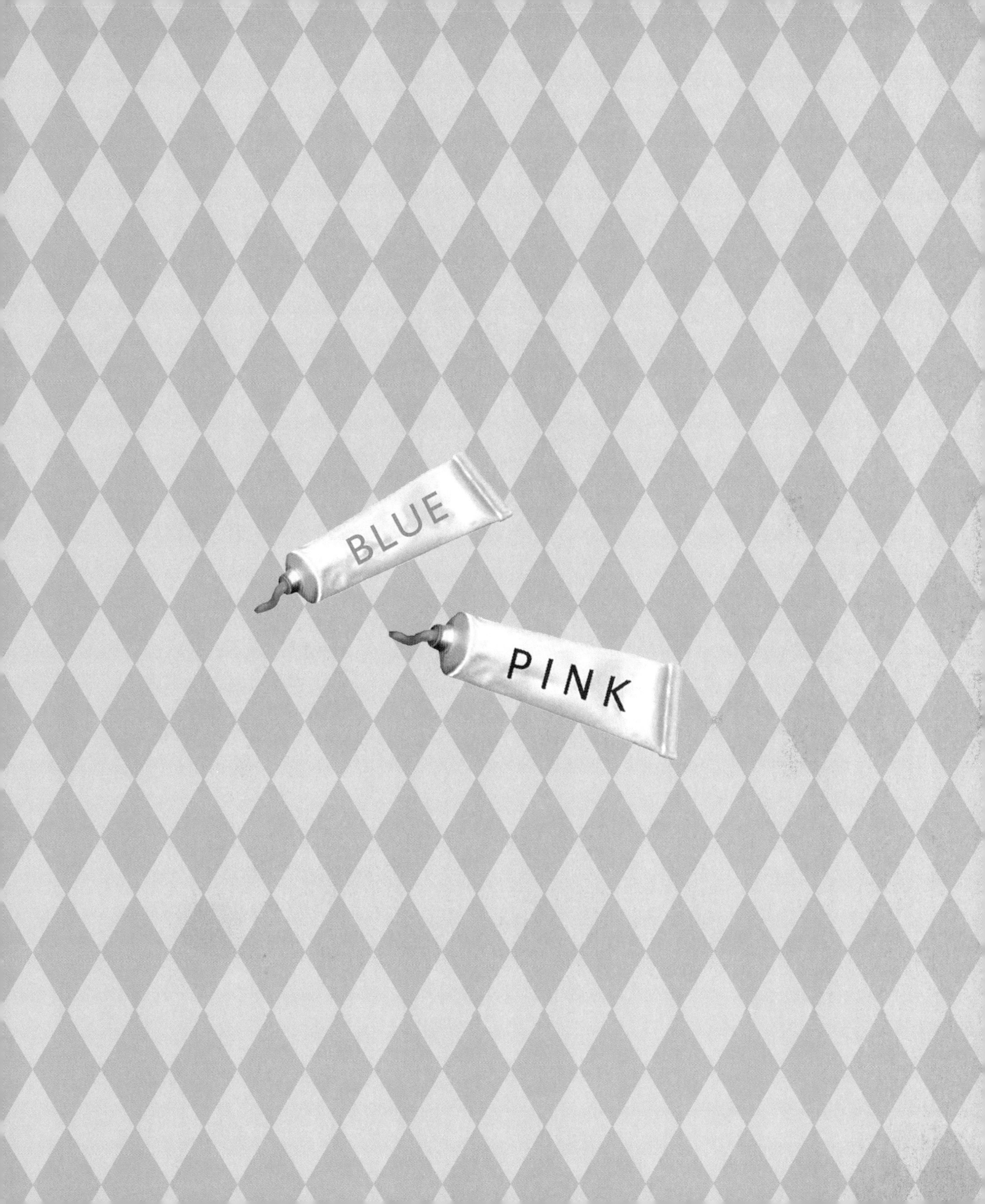
BLUE
PINK

Link arms
with a friend
and head straight
toward the fun!

Pinkie Promise: The Play

To put on a great play, you don't need a lot of props.
You just need a good story, and a lot of imagination!

Characters: Pinkalicious, Alison, Mr. Pushkin

Optional props*: paint set, piece of paper, jelly sandwich, paint tube, ice-cream cone.

*Remember: these props are optional. Pretending to use them works just as well!

Scene One

Setting: Classroom

Characters: Pinkalicious, Mr. Pushkin, Alison

ALISON: What are you making, Pinkalicious?

PINKALICIOUS: I'm making a picture for Mr. Pushkin. Oh no—I'm all out of pink! Can I borrow your paint set, Alison?

ALISON: Sure. Just don't use up all the pink, Pinkalicious!

PINKALICIOUS: I won't. I promise.

Pinkalicious paints.

PINKALICIOUS: Here, Mr. Pushkin! This painting is for you.

MR. PUSHKIN: What a terrific painting! It's so pink.

PINKALICIOUS: You mean it's pinkerrific!

ALISON: Can I have my paint set back now, Pinkalicious?

PINKALICIOUS: Um.… I'm sorry, Alison. By mistake I used up all the pink.

ALISON: You also used up all the red and the white.

PINKALICIOUS: Well, red and white make pink, so really it's all pink.

ALISON: You said you wouldn't use up all the pink paint!
You promised.

PINKALICIOUS: I'm really, really sorry, Alison.

Alison stomps away.

Scene Two

Setting: Lunchtime. Pinkalicious is sitting alone.

Characters: Pinkalicious, Mr. Pushkin

MR. PUSHKIN: Is everything okay, Pinkalicious?

PINKALICIOUS: My jelly sandwich doesn't taste
pink-a-yummy.

MR. PUSHKIN: Maybe your jelly sandwich doesn't
taste so pink-a-yummy because
you don't feel so pinkerrific.

PINKALICIOUS: Maybe.

Mr. Pushkin walks away.

PINKALICIOUS (to herself): I think I know
how to feel pinkerrific again. I'll make Alison
a card to apologize!

Scene Three

<u>Setting:</u> Back in the classroom   **<u>Characters:</u>** Pinkalicious, Alison

PINKALICIOUS: I made this card for you, Alison. It's very blue. There were no other colors. Almost everybody is out of pink.

ALISON: Thanks for the card. It's not just beautiful, it's bluetiful!

PINKALICIOUS: Alison, can we still be friends?

ALISON: Of course we're friends, Pinkalicious. I'm sorry I got angry about the paint. I won't get so mad next time.

Pinkalicious and Alison hug.

PINKALICIOUS: Let's play this weekend!

Scene Four

<u>Setting:</u> Pinkalicious's house and the ice-cream shop

<u>Characters:</u> Pinkalicious, Alison

PINKALICIOUS: This new tube of paint is for you, Alison.

ALISON: It's not even my birthday!

PINKALICIOUS: And that's not all. Guess what?

ALISON: What?

PINKALICIOUS: We're getting ice cream!

Pinkalicious and Alison walk to the ice-cream shop, and stop at the counter.

PINKALICIOUS: We'll split a pink peppermint ice-cream sundae with raspberry swirl syrup.

ALISON: And two cherries on top!

PINKALICIOUS: Some things are just too hard to share.

ALISON: Let's always be friends, Pinkalicious.

PINKALICIOUS: Yes, that would be fantastic. No, better than fantastic: it would be *pinkatastic*!

PINKALICIOUS AND ALISON: Let's make it a pinkie promise!

PINKALICIOUS: Pinkie promises last forever.

The End

Pinkie Rebuses

Figure out these phrases by following the picture clues!

1. Why did Pinkalicious use all of Alison's pink paint?

+ + PINK

2. How did Pinkalicious paint Alison's card?

WITH + **A** + − 🦷

3. What did Alison say to Pinkalicious during their playdate?

+ +

4. What did Pinkalicious and Alison have on their ice-cream sundae?

+ + **syrup**

Spot the Differences:
Art Time

Can you find 5 differences between the 2 pictures?

The End!